MW01569328

WITHDRAWN

EARTHQUAKES
Earth's Power

David and Patricia Armentrout

Publishing LLC
Vero Beach, Florida 32964

© 2007 Rourke Publishing LLC

All rights reserved. No part of this book may be reproduced or utilized in any form or by any means, electronic or mechanical including photocopying, recording, or by any information storage and retrieval system without permission in writing from the publisher.

www.rourkepublishing.com

PHOTO CREDITS: Cover, Title pg, pgs 6, 6 inset, 14, 25 inset courtesy of FEMA; Pgs 25, 27 courtesy of the Department of Defense; Pgs 5 inset, 10, 12 courtesy of USAID; Pg 18 courtesy of NOAA/Department of Commerce; Pg 22 inset courtesy of USDA; Pgs 13, 29 courtesy of the U.S. Department of the Interior, U.S. Geological Survey/C. E. Meyer; Pg 5 courtesy of the U.S. Department of the Interior, U.S. Geological Survey/G. K. Gilbert; Pg 21 inset courtesy of the U.S. Department of the Interior, U.S. Geological Survey/P. E. Hotz; Pgs 14 inset, 16, 17, 21, 22, 26 courtesy of the U.S. Department of the Interior, U.S. Geological Survey

Title page: Historical structures are left in ruins after a California earthquake.

Editor: Robert Stengard-Olliges

Cover and page design by Nicola Stratford

Library of Congress Cataloging-in-Publication Data

Armentrout, David, 1962-
 Earthquakes / David and Patricia Armentrout.
   p. cm. -- (Earth's power)
  ISBN 1-60044-230-7 (hardcover)
  ISBN 978-1-60044-339-8 (paperback)
  1. Earthquakes--Juvenile literature. I. Armentrout, Patricia, 1960- II. Title. III. Series: Armentrout, David, 1962- Earth's power.

 QE521.3.A757 2007
 551.22--dc22

2006011092

Printed in the USA

Rourke Publishing

www.rourkepublishing.com – sales@rourkepublishing.com
Post Office Box 3328, Vero Beach, FL 32964

TABLE OF CONTENTS

What is an Earthquake? 4
A Destructive Force of Nature 7
A Look Inside 8
Earthquake Science 11
Earthquake Scientists 15
The Richter Scale 19
San Francisco Quake 20
New Madrid Quake 23
Human Disasters 24
The Future of Earthquakes 28
Glossary 30
Further reading 31
Websites to Visit 31
Index 32

WHAT IS AN EARTHQUAKE?

The world around us is in constant motion, but the ground feels stable. It can be quite a shock when we are reminded that the earth is not as solid as it seems. An earthquake is the sudden and sometimes violent movement of the earth's surface caused by shifting rock inside the earth.

Those who have experienced an earthquake know the strange and uncomfortable feeling of moving earth.

Supplies are distributed in Pakistan after a magnitude 7.6 earthquake hit October 8, 2005.

The powerful 1906 San Francisco earthquake knocked this train off its track.

Damages from the 1994 Northridge, California quake were estimated at 25 billion dollars.

Homes and other personal property are destroyed in a landslide as a result of an earthquake.

A Destructive Force of Nature

Did you know that thousands of earthquakes occur every day? Fortunately, most are very small and cannot be felt. Big earthquakes are not nearly so common, but when one strikes, it can bring terrible devastation.

Earthquakes cause many problems. Ground shaking can knock buildings down and destroy roads and bridges. Vibrating earth can cause entire mountainsides to give way, creating **landslides** that destroy everything in their paths. Undersea earthquakes sometimes bring about monster waves called **tsunamis**. Tsunamis can travel over the ocean for thousands of miles causing death and destruction far from the earthquake.

2004-Sumatra: The powerful undersea earthquake that occurred off the coast of Sumatra, Indonesia in 2004 was devastating. The quake generated a giant tsunami that killed more than 280,000 people and destroyed property in more than 20 countries.

A LOOK INSIDE

The earth's interior is composed of three main layers, the **crust**, the **mantle,** and the **core**. The thin surface layer, or crust, is not one solid piece. It is made up of giant, slowly moving sections of rock called **tectonic plates**. The plates glide very slowly across the mantle, or middle layer. The mantle is made mostly of white-hot, semi-**molten** rock called **magma**. Scientists believe earth's center, or core, is mostly iron.

Breaks or cracks in the earth's crust are known as faults. Most earthquakes occur along fault lines and near the boundaries or edges of tectonic plates.

```
Tectonic plates
move only about
as fast as
fingernails grow,
roughly two
inches a year.
```

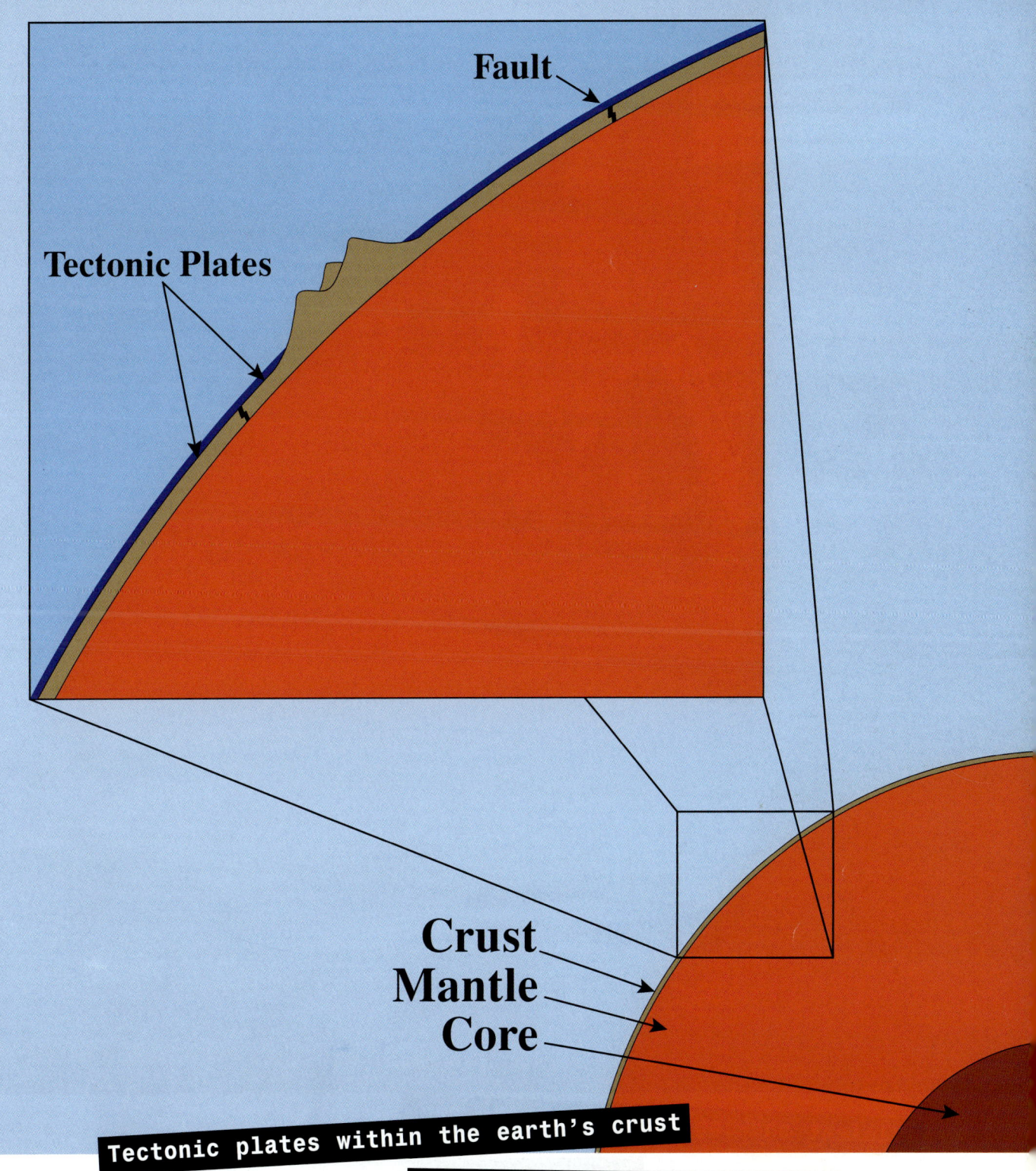

Tectonic plates within the earth's crust slowly move across the mantle.

Violent shaking during a quake can cause roadways to break apart.

EARTHQUAKE SCIENCE

Magma and other forces deep within the earth push along tectonic plates. Sometimes friction causes the plates or sections of a plate to stick. However, the forces moving the plates do not stop. These forces press the plates tighter and tighter against each other. Over a long time, sometimes thousands of years, pressure builds to the breaking point. Eventually the stress overcomes the friction and the plates slip past each other or break. Built-up energy is released suddenly, causing an earthquake. The point where this occurs is called the **focus**. The energy travels away from the focus in waves. The waves cause the ground to shake.

The **epicenter** is the location on the surface directly above an earthquake's focus. When an earthquake occurs, scientists work quickly to pinpoint the epicenter. This is important because the epicenter is often where the worst damage occurs.

1556-Shansi, China:

It is difficult to say which natural disaster has taken the greatest toll in human lives. It is certain, however, that the earthquake that struck the Shansi province of China was one of the most destructive in world history. It is estimated that 830,000 people died as a result of the powerful earthquake.

Emergency health kits are loaded on a plane to be distributed to earthquake survivors in Pakistan.

The 1989 Loma Prieta earthquake caused major damage to the the San Francisco Bay area.

Core samples taken from deep inside the earth are examined.

A house sits lopsided on its foundation after a magnitude 6.7 quake hit near Los Angeles.

EARTHQUAKE SCIENTISTS

Seismologists are scientists who study earthquakes. A seismologist measures an earthquake's strength or **magnitude**. It is easy to see and measure damage caused by an earthquake, but measuring its magnitude is tricky. A powerful earthquake in an unpopulated area will cause less damage than a weaker one that strikes near a city.

1960-Chile:
The earthquake that occurred off the coast of Chile in 1960 was the largest ever recorded. More than 2000 people died and thousands more were injured. Entire villages were leveled. Buildings and homes collapsed. Many died under massive landslides. A giant tsunami caused death and destruction along both sides of the Pacific Ocean.

Seismologists use an instrument called a seismograph to detect vibrations in the earth. These vibrations, or waves of energy, are seismic waves. Seismologists can tell how strong an earthquake is by studying seismic waves.

Seismographs record vibrations within the earth.

Italian Luigi Palmieri created the first seismograph in 1855. Palmieri's device recorded the time, strength, and duration of an earthquake.

A giant drill bores into an active section of the San Andreas Fault in California. Seismic instruments will be placed in the hole to observe fault activity.

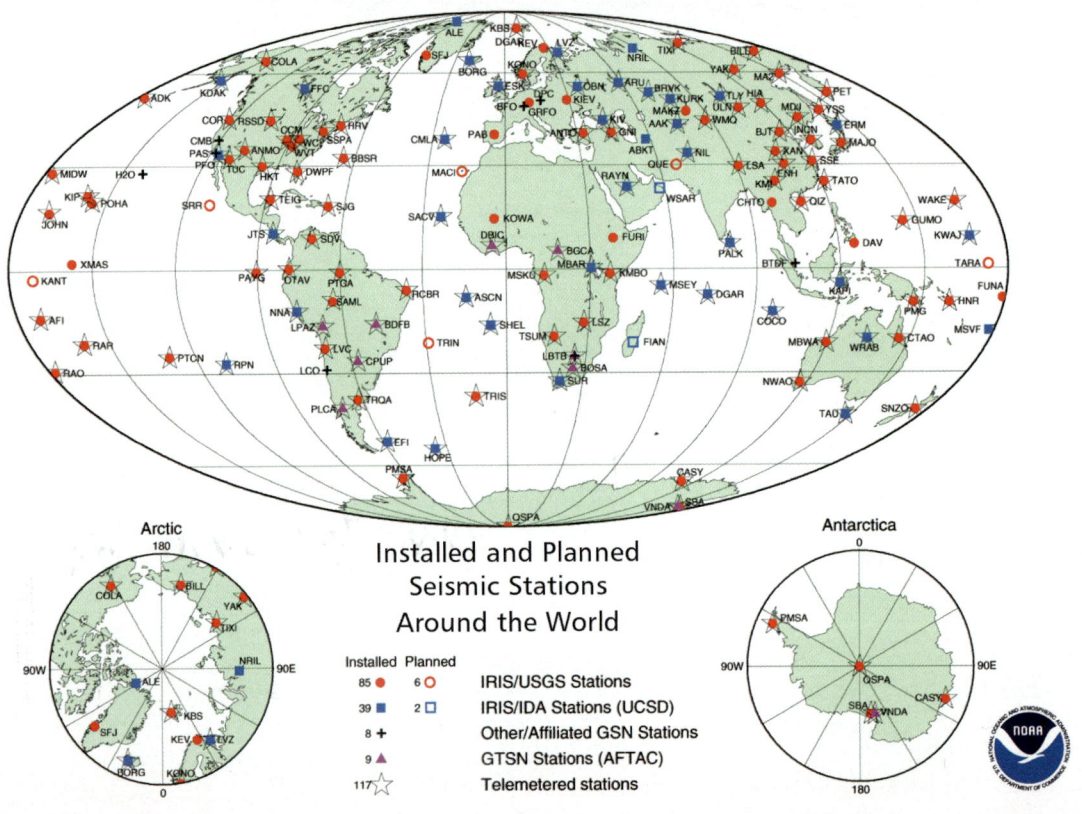

Installed and Planned Seismic Stations Around the World

Installed	Planned	
85 ●	6 ○	IRIS/USGS Stations
39 ■	2 □	IRIS/IDA Stations (UCSD)
8 +		Other/Affiliated GSN Stations
9 ▲		GTSN Stations (AFTAC)
117 ☆		Telemetered stations

EARTHQUAKE MAGNITUDE SCALE

Magnitude	Effects	Estimated Number Each Year Worldwide
8.0 or greater	Great earthquake. Catastrophic damage possible over large area.	1 or less
7.0-7.9	Major earthquake. Serious damage	17
6.0-6.9	Strong earthquake. Heavy damage to populated areas.	120
5.0-5.9	Moderate earthquake. Slight damage to buildings and other structures.	800
4.0-4.9	Light earthquake. Minor damage possible.	6,200
3.9 or less	Minor and very minor earthquakes. The largest may be felt near the epicenter, but generally produce little if any damage.	1,430,000.

THE RICHTER SCALE

Charles Richter was an American seismologist. In 1935, he developed the Richter Scale to measure an earthquake's size. Although a new, more accurate method known as the Moment Magnitude Scale is sometimes used to measure earthquakes, the Richter Scale remains the most well known. Each whole number increase on the Richter Scale is equal to a ten-fold increase in an earthquake's size. For example, a quake that registers 7.5 on the Richter Scale would create ten times more ground shaking than a quake that registers 6.5.

1976-Tangshan, China:

The official death toll from the 1976 earthquake in Tangshan, China stands at 255,000, but most experts agree it may have been as high as 655,000. The entire city was destroyed. The quake hit suddenly during the early morning hours. Collapsing homes crushed many victims while they slept.

SAN FRANCISCO QUAKE

The 1906 earthquake that hit San Francisco, California was the deadliest earthquake in U.S. history. The earthquake occurred along an active fault line known as the San Andreas Fault. The quake was not the largest, but it caused terrible damage and loss of life. Several thousand people died and hundreds of thousands were left homeless.

Although the quake caused considerable damage, the disaster was made much worse by fires that spread across the city shortly after. Many of the city's water mains were ruptured during the quake. The lack of water made it almost impossible for firefighters to control the blazes. In the end, fires may have caused more damage than the earthquake.

San Francisco residents watch as the city burns after the 1906 quake.

Shaking during the 1906 San Francisco quake caused a statue to fall from its rooftop piercing the sidewalk 30 feet below.

Reelfoot Lake, Tennessee.

Tree twisted by the violent shaking of the New Madrid quake.

NEW MADRID QUAKE

The largest earthquake recorded in the continental U.S. happened in 1812. The quake was centered near the town of New Madrid in what is now Missouri. It was felt hundreds of miles away. The jolt was powerful enough to ring church bells in Boston, 1200 miles to the east.

The New Madrid earthquake caused major damage to many small towns near the epicenter. Fortunately, the area was not heavily populated then. A quake of this magnitude today could be catastrophic.

Reelfoot Lake in western Tennessee was created when the New Madrid earthquake caused a huge section of land to sink. The newly created basin eventually filled with water.

HUMAN DISASTERS

A powerful earthquake strikes somewhere in the world almost every year. Why do some earthquakes cause more damage than others do? Why do some earthquakes turn into human tragedy? Certainly size and location are two factors, but there are other reasons.

Natural disasters turn into human disasters when people die needlessly. Large human disasters are more likely in poor, less developed nations that lack money and resources. Buildings are often poorly constructed and safety standards may not exist. Human disasters are also more likely in remote areas where rescue and relief assistance is very difficult.

A search and rescue squad inspects earthquake damage in Iran.

Soldiers unload supplies for earthquake victims.

The waterfront along Kodiak, Alaska was destroyed by the 1964 tsunami.

A powerful quake rattled the earth in Pakistan in 2005. Officials estimate that 80,000 people died. Unfortunately, many perished from hunger, disease, and lack of medical attention after the quake. Dozens of nations sent help, but rough terrain, bad weather, and landslides that blocked mountain roads slowed rescue efforts.

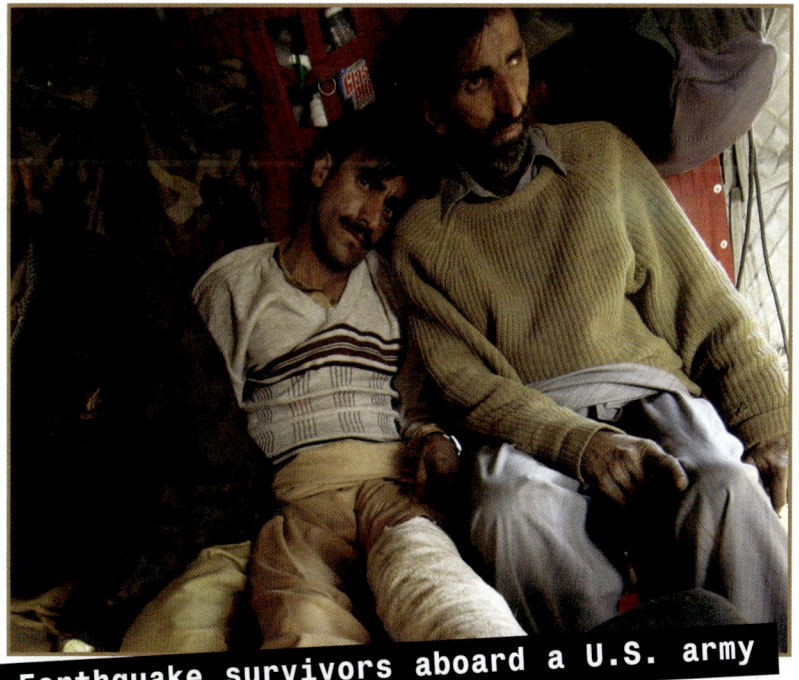

Earthquake survivors aboard a U.S. army helicopter are airlifted to Pakistan for medical attention.

1964-Prince William Sound, Alaska:

The most powerful earthquake ever recorded in the United States occurred in Alaska. The quake measured 8.6 on the Richter Scale and 9.2 on the Moment Magnitude Scale. Huge landslides triggered tsunamis that killed more than 100 people in Alaska. The tsunamis traveled hundreds of miles across open ocean killing coastal residents as far away as California and Oregon.

THE FUTURE OF EARTHQUAKES

It is not likely that scientists will ever find a way to prevent earthquakes. But that does not mean people cannot find ways to reduce damage and protect lives.

Seismologists will get better at predicting where and when an earthquake will happen. With advance notice, people will have time to seek safe shelter. **Architects** and **engineers** are already designing earthquake resistant buildings, bridges, and roads. These improvements will not eliminate earthquakes, but will reduce the terrible toll that earthquakes take.

Collapsed bridge span on the San Francisco-Oakland Bay Bridge.

GLOSSARY

architect (ARE ki tekt) — someone who designs buildings

core (KOR) — the intensely hot, center section of the earth

crust (KRUHST) — the hard outer layer of the earth

epicenter (EP uh sent ur) — the area directly above an earthquake's focus

engineers (en juh NIHRZ) — people trained to design and build roads, bridges, and other structures

focus (FOH kuhs) — the point in the earth where an earthquake occurs

landslides (LAND slidez) — sudden movement of earth and rock down mountains or hills

magma (MAG muh) — melted rock below the earth's surface

magnitude (MAG nuh tood) — term used to describe the scale or size of an earthquake

mantle (MAN tuhl) — the layer of the earth between the crust and core

molten (MOHLT uhn) — melted by heat

tectonic plates (tek TON ik PLAYT) — sections of the earth's crust

tsunamis (soo NAH meez) — large waves caused by an underwater earthquake or volcano

FURTHER READING

Van Rose, Susanna. *Volcano & Earthquake.* DK Publishing, Inc, 2004.

Reed, Jennifer. *Earthquakes, Disaster and Survival.* Enslow Publishers, Inc, 2005.

Simon, Seymour. *Earthquakes.* HarperCollins, 2006.

WEBSITES TO VISIT

USGS
http://earthquake.usgs.gov/learning/kids.php

FEMA For Kids
http://www.fema.gov/kids/quake.htm

Howstuffworks
http://www.howstuffworks.com/earthquake.htm

INDEX

Chile 15
fault 8
fires 20
moment magnitude scale 19
New Madrid 20
Pakistan 27
Palmieri, Luigi 16
Prince William Sound 27
Richter scale 19
rock 4
San Andreas Fault 20
San Francisco 20
Shansi 12
Sumatra 7
seismic waves 16
seismologist 15, 16, 19, 28
Tangshan 19
tectonic plates 8, 11
tsunami 7
undersea 7

ABOUT THE AUTHORS

David and Patricia Armentrout have written many nonfiction books for young readers. They have had several books published for primary school reading. The Armentrouts live in Cincinnati, Ohio, with their two children.